For Gaëlle,
and for Jacques

Orchard Books, 95 Madison Avenue, New York, NY 10016

Manufactured in France   Book design by Mina Greenstein
The text of this book is set in 18 point Veljovic Medium.
The illustrations are watercolor paintings reproduced
in full color.   2   3   4   5   6   7   8   9   10

Library of Congress Cataloging-in-Publication Data
Davenier, Christine.
[Léon et Albertine. English]
Leon and Albertine / by Christine Davenier ; [translated by
Dominic Barth]. — 1st American ed.   p.   cm.
Summary: Leon the pig follows the advice of the other barn-
yard animals in trying to get the attention of Albertine the
chicken, with whom he has fallen in love.
ISBN 0-531-30072-2
[1. Pigs—Fiction. 2. Chickens—Fiction. 3. Domestic
animals—Fiction.] I. Title.
PZ7.D2735Lg 1998 [E]—dc21 97-25399

Christine Davenier

Leon and Albertine

Orchard Books   New York

Leon followed the same routine each morning. It was simple: wallow in a mud puddle with good friends. In short, Leon led the life of a happy pig.

But after he fell in love, his life became a disaster. The wonderful chicken, Albertine, invaded his every thought and deed. What could he do to get her to notice him?
Poor Leon! He was desperate.
Nothing else mattered to him.
He decided to ask
his friends' advice.

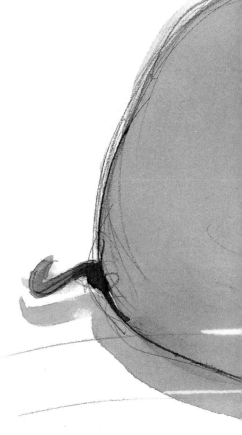

ocorico

"The best way to get a
chicken's attention,"
proclaimed the rooster,
"is to sing."

But Albertine snored so loudly
that she could not hear
Leon's serenade.

"Dance, dance, dance," advised the rabbit gaily.
"That always works!"

But Albertine pecked ceaselessly
without raising her head.

"How do you expect to appeal to Albertine with your pig's fashion sense?" asked the turkey. "Do something about your appearance and she'll notice you."

But Albertine was too preoccupied to pay attention to Leon.

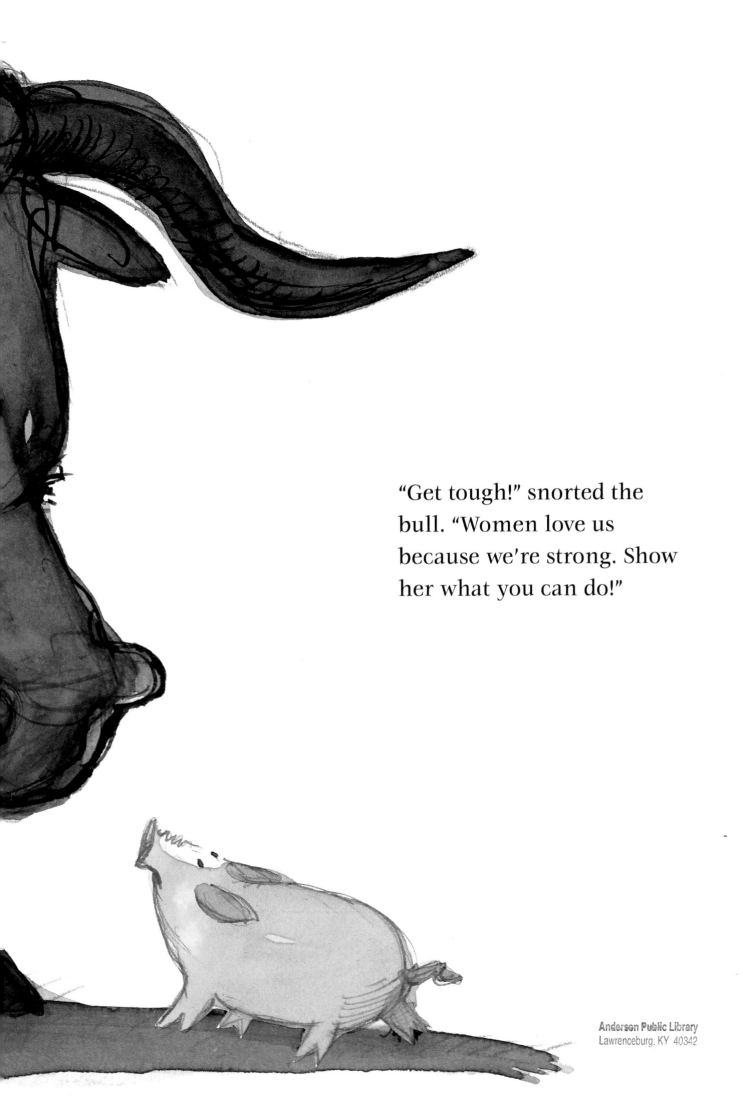

"Get tough!" snorted the bull. "Women love us because we're strong. Show her what you can do!"

But Albertine was indifferent
to Leon's display of strength.

"What if you did
a spectacular dive into the lake?"
quacked the duck.

But Albertine was in
too much of a hurry
to admire Leon's
latest stunt.

It's pointless, Leon thought to himself,
on the verge of tears. I've tried everything.
Albertine will never notice me.
I give up.

"Hey, Leon," called his friend Gaston.
"Where are you going? Come play with me."

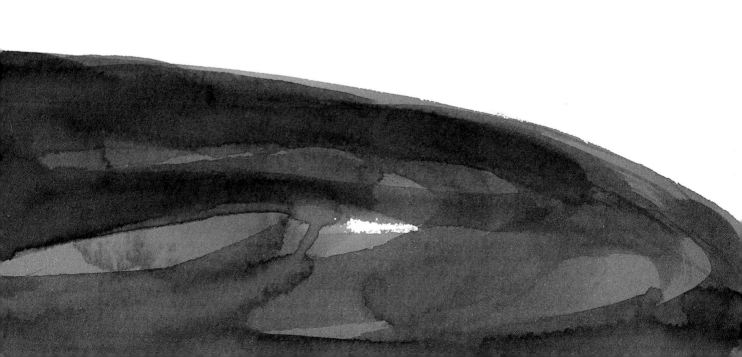

Leon sighed. "Oh, why not!"

He splashed into the mud.
The two buddies did somersaults,
pirouettes, cartwheels. They
laughed so hard that Leon forgot
his sadness.

Their joy was contagious:
soon all the farm animals were
splashing in the mud.

Suddenly, Leon stopped. He couldn't believe his eyes. Albertine was right in front of him, looking at him, smiling.

"Oh, Leon!" she said. "I've had so much fun with you! I'd love to do it all over again."

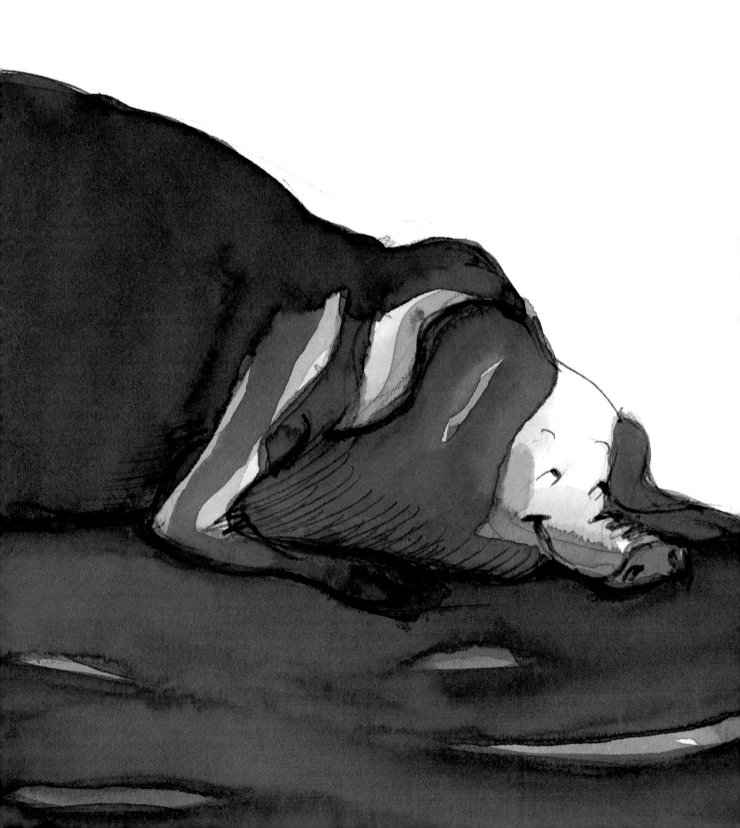

Leon took a deep breath. He closed his eyes.
And, without asking anyone's advice,
he whispered, "I love you, Albertine."